11.00 County

D0368537

JF HUT

Skate, Robyn, Skate!

by Hazel Hutchins

Illustrated by Yvonne Cathcart

First Novels

The New Series

Formac Publishing Company Limited
Halifax

Formac Publishing Company Limited acknowledges the support of the Cultural Affairs Section, Nova Scotia Department of Tourism and Culture. We acknowledge the financial support of the Government of Canada through the Book Publishing Industry Development Program (BPIDP) for our publishing activities.

We acknowledge the support of the Canada Council for the Arts for our publishing program.

National Library of Canada Cataloguing in Publication Data

Hutchins, H. J. (Hazel J.)
    Skate, Robyn, skate / by Hazel Hutchins ; illustrated by Yvonne Cathcart.

(First novels ; 30)
ISBN 0-88780-627-9 (bound).—ISBN 0-88780-626-0 (pbk.)

    I. Cathcart, Yvonne II. Title. III. Series.

PS8565.U826S55 2004   jC813'.54   C2004-900554-5

Formac Publishing Company Limited
5502 Atlantic Street
Halifax, Nova Scotia, B3H 1G4
www.formac.ca

Distributed in the United States by:
Orca Book Publishers
P.O. Box 468 Custer, WA
USA 98240-0468

Printed and bound in Canada

Table of Contents

*To Gay, Dorothy and
Anna with hugs and thanks*

1
Robyn Rules

"Go, go, go!"

My best friend Marie shot across the ice. That's how Marie skates — fast. Marie plays hockey with her brothers.

"Bend your knees! Push with your legs!" she called.

She shot past me again. Marie says her brothers drive her crazy, but when it comes to skating she's as crazy as they are.

"Do cross-overs! Take the corner!"

Marie was helping me learn

to skate better. It wasn't working. Marie had hockey skates — her very own hockey skates. I had figure skates — borrowed figure skates, two sizes too large. The way Marie skated, her whole body moved together. The way I skated, every part of me felt like it was out of place.

I pushed ...or at least I thought I did.

I crossed ...or at least I tried to.

I caught the toe pick of my skate on a bump and went sprawling across the ice. Marie raced over and did one of those instant hockey stops. "Are you okay?" she asked.

Marie and her brothers have what they call Hockey Rules. Unless your leg is

broken in three places, you have to say you're fine. "I'm fine," I said.

"You have to keep low," said Marie. "You have to bend your knees."

I couldn't help it. I glared at her. I'd heard it all, way too many times.

"Maybe you should just practise on your own for a while," sighed Marie.

When I skate on my own I use Robyn Rules. No cornering. No cross-overs.

No fancy sliding stops — not that I can do them anyway. When I want to stop, I skate into the ridge of packed snow at the side of the pond. I smile while I'm doing it so everyone will think I'm stopping that way just for fun.

I skated across the pond and stopped in the snow. I skated back again and stopped in the snow. I smiled. Skating is easy if you use your own rules. I even began to hum along with the music.

Hummmm-tee-tee-tummmm-tee-tee-tummmmm.

And then a little faster.

Humm-te-te-tumm-te...

And then faster.

Hum-te-tum-te-tum-te-...

Too fast! Too fast! I shot right through the little ridge of snow and landed — *fwoosh* — in the bank beyond.

"At least you're still smiling," said Marie.

My face muscles had frozen that way.

2
Farting Feathers

I smiled all the way home. It takes a long time to thaw out after you've been skating on the pond and you are frozen clear through. Besides, if I stopped smiling I was going to be really mad and scream.

"I used to smile like that," said Mrs. Kelly. "I take it the skating didn't go very well."

Mrs. Kelly lives in the apartment next door to Mom and me. She had loaned me the skates.

"Come in and warm up while I tell you about my own

skating adventures," said Mrs. Kelly. "The twins and I could use some company."

The twins are Abigail and Angie. I help Mr. and Mrs. Kelly look after them. I like the twins, and just playing with them makes me feel better. Mrs. Kelly made hot chocolate to warm me up. It felt good to be able to move my face muscles again.

"When I first tried to skate, I was younger than you, Robyn — just a little girl really," said Mrs. Kelly. "Even then, I remember how mad I used to get. My brothers and sisters went zooming around the ice. All I did was fall on my bottom. I fell so many times that my

mom began to worry that I was going to hurt myself.

"So what she did ...," Mrs. Kelly stopped. A funny look came over her face. "I don't think I've ever actually told anyone this. It's kind of embarrassing."

"What?" I asked. "What did she do?"

"She sewed a pillow to the seat of my snowpants," said Mrs. Kelly. "Whenever I fell, feathers went flying into the air. It was like ...," she began to giggle, "It was like I was farting feathers."

We were still rolling on the carpet laughing when Mr. Kelly came home.

3
Gliders, Sliders ... and Robyn

Laughter is really good for making you feel better, but it doesn't help you learn to skate. I wanted to learn to skate. I was tired of crashing all the time. I didn't want anyone to think I needed a pillow!

Private lessons are for kids who want to be in competitions. They cost a lot of money. We don't have a lot of money. Luckily, I saw an ad for group lessons at the indoor rink. Mom said we could afford them if I could live without renting videos for a while.

Going to my first *anything* makes me nervous. When I got to the rink there were about a zillion kids of different ages. A lady came out and began to organize things.

"*Gliders* down at the far end," she said and pointed.

"*Sliders* between the blue lines," she said and pointed to the hockey stripes on the ice.

I was still waiting with two girls a grade younger than I am and a bunch of really little kids. That was okay. I could learn to skate with two girls a grade younger.

"Brit, Jody, pay attention please!" said the lady. "You're Sliders."

The two girls left. I didn't want to learn to skate with a bunch of little kids!

That's when something good happened. Jessica Johnson appeared from the change rooms down the hall. Jessica Johnson is in my grade and she walked right into our group. Hurrah!

It wasn't until she began printing out name tags that I realized why she was there.

4
Learning to Fall

Jessica wasn't taking lessons, she was helping to teach them!

"The kids in private lessons help the beginners," she said. "I'm in private lessons."

It figures. Jessica's family has a lot of money.

I looked around. Maybe I could get a different teacher. But ... "It's good that you've got me," said Jessica, "because Ms. Grimes is the crabbiest teacher around."

Couldn't *anything* go right?

"Quick, quick," said the

crabbiest teacher around. "Everyone on the ice."

The little kids and I trooped onto the ice. We could all skate a bit, but most of us kept one hand on the boards just in case. One kid even fell — *plop* — right on his bottom. *Feather fart*, I thought, but I didn't giggle. I knew how he felt.

Jessica didn't troop. She glided. She spun. She spread her arms and did a twisting jump. I almost left right then and there.

"Jessica, quit showing off," spoke up Ms. Grimes. "Show these kids how to fall."

Jessica looked my way and rolled her eyes.

"Quick, quick," said Ms.

Grimes. She was already beginning to sound crabbier.

Jessica did a sliding kind of fall. We all tried to do the same thing. Sliding falls are easier on you than feather farts, but they're still falling. I already knew that part of skating.

After that, Jessica showed us pie stops. Pie stops are when you push out on the back of your skates and make a triangle with your feet, like a piece of pie. I didn't want to learn how to do pie stops. I wanted to do hockey stops.

For the rest of the lesson Jessica showed us bubbles and bunny hops. Just the names of the moves made me feel about three years old.

That was it. Time to take the skates back to Mrs. Kelly for good.

5
Showing Mrs. Kelly

"The marshmallow monster leaps — *boing, boing, boing* — across the table, and plops into the hot chocolate!"

The twins giggled. It doesn't take much to make the twins giggle, and that's another thing I like about them. Of course their chocolate was mostly milk and was only a little bit warm. My hot chocolate was wonderfully hot and yummy.

"Robyn," said Mrs. Kelly. "I was wondering if I could ask you something a little bit crazy."

"Sure," I said.

"I know you said your lessons weren't much fun, " said Mrs. Kelly. "But I was wondering … do you think you could teach me what you learn?"

I looked at Mrs. Kelly. Was this some kind of adult trick to get me back to lessons? I didn't think so. Mrs. Kelly isn't that kind of adult.

"But you already know how to skate," I said.

"No, I don't," she said. "I never did learn."

"Because of feather farts?" I asked.

Mrs. Kelly shook her head.

"I'm just not very co-ordinated," she said. "My brothers and sisters picked it up by playing on the pond, like your friend Marie, but I never got the hang of it."

"But you have your own skates," I said. "Even now."

"I always *wanted* to learn," she said. "I always *planned* on taking lessons. I never quite did it. It's embarrassing to take lessons when you're an adult and little kids can skate better than you."

I knew how she felt.

I tried to show her pie stops, bubbles, and bunny hops on the kitchen floor. It didn't work very well. Mrs. Kelly looked disappointed. I couldn't disappoint Mrs. Kelly.

Saturday morning, before it got busy, we went down to

the pond. I showed her as best I could on the ice. It's easier to try to do things when no one is around.

After that, I took off the skates and Mrs. Kelly put them on. She even put on a helmet. I watched the twins while she tried sliding falls, bubbles, and bunny hops.

The next Wednesday, I went back to lessons. In fact, I went for the next six weeks. Lessons still weren't much fun with a bunch of little kids, a crabby teacher, and Jessica sneaking off to practise her own jumps and loops. But showing Mrs. Kelly was fun.

And then I found out about the Carnival.

6
Getting Ready for the Carnival

The Carnival is like *Stars on Ice*. The Carnival is like *Ice Capades*. There are costumes, spotlights, music, and lots of people who come to watch. Everyone in skating lessons has to be in the Carnival because it helps to raise money for the skating club. That's what Ms. Grimes told us.

If you're a Slider or a Glider it's probably fun. If you're a Beginner — especially a Beginner in a group with a bunch of little kids — it's a disaster.

The theme of the Carnival this year was Other Lands. Ms. Grimes had chosen Mexico for our group. We would wear ponchos and sombreros. We would do the world's slowest Mexican Hat Dance and skate in straight lines.

Ms. Grimes became crabbier and crabbier as she tried to get everyone to do things at the right time. I wasn't much help. I *could* do everything — in fact, I could do it better than the little kids — but I didn't want to.

"What do you mean you don't want to be in the Carnival?" said Marie enviously. "Hockey players never get carnivals."

Hockey players get world tournaments and Stanley Cups.

"We'll sew lots of sparkles on your costume," said my mom. "Everyone will say *ohhh* and *ahhh* and won't notice that you're way older than everyone else."

The world didn't have enough sparkles for that to happen.

At lessons, we began to practise one group at a time on the ice. I sat with the Beginners and watched the Sliders. Their teacher had thought of a way to make good use of the fact that Brit and Jody were older and taller than the rest. They had ribbons that they swirled above the little kids. They also had each other.

"You know, Robyn, you're almost good enough to be in the Slider group," said Jessica Johnson.

She was sitting beside me wearing a fancy white fur hat. Jessica was skating her own routine to music from Russia.

"Do you think their teacher would let me?" I asked.

"Nope," said Jessica. "Sliders have to be able to stop."

"I can stop," I said.

"You can pie stop," said Jessica. "Sliders have to be able to hockey stop."

I knew I was learning the wrong stuff!

That day, when we finally hit the ice, I was the kid in the sombrero who fell over all the time because she was trying to do hockey stops instead of pie stops. The teacher looked crabbier than ever by the time it was over.

7
New Skates

Saturday morning, Mrs. Kelly
had a surprise for me. My
own skates!

"I told my sister that you
were teaching me," said Mrs.
Kelly. "This is a pair that her
own kids have outgrown. I'm

pretty sure they'll fit. I've had them sharpened for you. I hope you don't mind that they're second-hand."

I didn't mind. They looked great!

"Wow," I said. "Thanks!"

"Now we'll be able to skate together," said Mrs. Kelly.

"And when the twins get old enough, we'll both be able to help them," I said.

That morning, Mom went to the pond with us. She watched the twins while Mrs. Kelly and I skated together. It took me a while to get used to my new skates, but Mom was impressed by how much I'd learned.

"I'm glad you stuck with the lessons," said Mom at lunch.

"I'd be glad too, except for the Carnival," I said.

After lunch, I tried to phone Marie to tell her about my new skates. She wasn't home. I went back to the pond on my own just in case she was there.

A warm Chinook wind had blown in. Winter had disappeared and the sun was hot. People were skating without jackets on. The main pond was too busy for practising, so I skated down one of the side channels. Way at the end were some Danger signs, but I wasn't skating nearly that far.

Skate and stop. Skate and stop. For a while I got better — not a lot better, but a little better. If I kind of lifted first, I could push into the stop. My new skates seemed better than my old ones, they slid and bit at the same time — it's kind of hard to explain.

Pretty soon, however, I began to get tired. After that, all I did was get worse.

I was planning how to scrunch down under my sombrero and add a zillion sparkles to my poncho, when a couple of teenagers came skating a million miles an hour down the channel. They were calling back and forth, skating forwards and backwards, and having a great time. They *swooshed* right by me and on down past the signs.

And the next minute, I couldn't believe my eyes. They both went through the ice.

8
Robyn to the Rescue

It couldn't be happening!
People didn't fall through the
ice at the pond — the pond
was supposed to be safe. But
I'd seen it!

When someone falls
through the ice, the worst
thing you can do is fall in
yourself. If you're going to
help someone, you lie flat on
the ice. You throw something
to them. You make sure
you're big enough so they
don't pull you in.

I didn't have anything to
throw. They were bigger than

me. There were two of them. I needed help — fast!

Bend your knees, stay low, push hard.

I was finally good enough to understand what Marie had meant. I was even good enough not to catch my picks on the ice.

I raced down the channel, faster and faster. I rounded the corner. Turn, turn, turn.

And then all of a sudden I was around the corner and at the main pond and I was going a zillion miles an hour and there were people crossing in front of me everywhere.

"Help!" I called. "Help!"

People turned to look at me. I was going way too fast.

I had to stop or I'd run into them. I had to stop. Now!

I lifted. I pushed. My skates slid and bit all at once.

"Help!" I said. "Some people have gone through the ice!"

9
A Great Stop

I expected everyone to scream and spring into action. I expected everyone to race for ropes. I expected everyone to call ambulances and rescue helicopters. Instead, people began to talk in their everyday voices.

"It's not deep down there, is it?" asked an older man.

"No deeper than my knees," said a lady with a bright blue hat.

"Swampy more than anything else," said a man with a beard. "They might get their pants a bit wet."

"Unless they've hurt themselves by twisting an ankle," said the lady.

"I guess I'll mosey on down and make sure they're okay," said the older man.

"I'll come with you," said the lady.

They took off down the channel at a pleasant, friendly pace.

"You mean they aren't going to drown?" I asked the man with the beard. I had to be sure.

"They won't drown," he said. "But you did the right thing to let us know what happened."

I may have done the right thing, but I was going to feel

like a complete idiot as soon as my heart stopped going *thump, thump, thump.*

I didn't have time, however. The next moment someone came racing across the ice towards me with a great big grin on her face. It was Marie.

"Wow, Robyn, you sure have learned to skate! That was a great stop," she said.

Hey! She was right!

10
The Carnival

I didn't move up to Glider level. When you know you really *can* do something, you don't mind doing it with a bunch of little kids. Besides, I found out that Abigail and Angie were coming to the Carnival. They'd be able to spot me on the ice a whole lot easier among all the little kids in the Beginner group.

For our final practice, instead of messing up the Mexico routine by stopping all the time, I helped the little kids have fun — in spite of

crabby Ms. Grimes.

During some spare time, instead of being jealous of Jessica with her private lessons and furry hat, I got her to teach me flatirons and simple spins. It was going to take a lot more practice to learn them, but now I had something else to work on with Mrs. Kelly.

And the night of the Carnival itself, when they darkened the rink and turned on the spotlights so that all the sparkles glittered like a million stars, I didn't feel like I stood out after all. I felt like I was part of something magical.

"That's it," said Marie the next day at the pond. "I'm

going to sew sparkles on my hockey jersey."

"No, you're not," I told her.

"I'm going to get a white furry hat and learn to do jumps and spins," she said.

"No, you're not," I told her.

"I'm going to skate even faster and learn to puck handle and slapshot into the net," said Marie.

"Go, go, go!" I shouted.

Marie blasted off across the pond.

I followed ... a little bit — but *only* a little bit — behind.

Two more new novels in the *First Novels Series*

Lilly Makes a Friend

Brenda Bellingham
Illustrated by Clarke MacDonald

Lilly keeps getting into trouble at school whenever Davy, a boy from the kindergarten class, asks her for help. It's a new challenge for Lilly: Davy is blind and a lot smaller than her and her friends. His dream is to play soccer with the bigger boys and he wants to shoot a goal with Lilly as goalie. Lilly tries to distract him by teaching him to yodel. He persists and they find a way to play with Davy's special ball, but even this doesn't satisfy him. Everyone has an idea of what's best for Davy, even Lilly. But Davy has his own ideas about what he can and will do. *Lilly Makes a Friend* is a touching story that shows how integrating special-needs children into the schools is a challenge worth pursuing.

Morgan Makes a Splash

Ted Staunton
Illustrated by Bill Slavin

When Morgan starts swimming lessons, he has
lots of problems to deal with. There is the towel
flicking and the slimy floor in the change room.
There's the jiggles in his tummy he needs to
cover up with his t-shirt and the scary possibility
that his suit will drop to his knees when he
jumps in. Worst of all, Aldeen Hummell, the
Godzilla of Grade Three, has told him she will
turn him into cat food if he doesn't cover for her
while she plays hooky.

Once again Morgan finds himself dragged into
Aldeen's plans. But by playing the clown, and
facing his own fears, he thinks he can free
himself from her clasp by helping her get her
badge.

Morgan Makes a Splash is a hilarious story
about gathering courage to cope with difficult
situations.

Meet all the great kids in the *First Novels Series!*

Meet Duff
Duff's Monkey Business
Duff the Giant Killer

Meet Jan
Jan's Awesome Party
Jan on the Trail
Jan and Patch
Jan's Big Bang

Meet Lilly
Lilly in the Middle
Lilly's Clever Puppy
Lilly Plays Her Part
Lilly's Good Deed
Lilly to the Rescue

Meet Robyn
Robyn Makes the News
Robyn's Art Attack
Robyn's Best Idea
Robyn Looks for Bears
Robyn's Want Ad
Shoot for the Moon, Robyn

Meet Morgan
Morgan's Pet Plot
Morgan's Birthday
Great Play, Morgan
Morgan's Secret
Morgan and the Money
Morgan Makes Magic

Meet Carrie
Carrie Loses Her Nerve
Carrie's Camping Adventure
Carrie's Crowd
Go For It, Carrie

Meet Leo
Leo's Poster Challenge
Leo and Julio

Meet Marilou
Marilou Forecasts the Future
Marilou Cries Wolf
Marilou, Iguana Hunter
Marilou on Stage
Marilou's Long Nose

Meet Toby
Toby's Best Friend

Meet Maddie
Maddie on TV
Maddie's Millionaire Dreams
Maddie Needs Her Own Life
Maddie Wants New Clothes
Maddie Tries to be Good
Maddie in Trouble
Maddie in Hospital
Maddie in Goal
Maddie in Danger
Maddie Goes to Paris
Maddie Wants Music
That's Enough Maddie

Meet Arthur
Arthur Throws a Tantrum
Arthur's Dad
Arthur's Problem Puppy

Meet Fred
Fred's Halloween Adventure
Fred on the Ice Floes
Fred and the Food
Fred and the Stinky Cheese
Fred's Dream Cat
Fred's Midnight Prowler

Meet Mikey

Mikey Mite's Best Present
Good For You, Mikey Mite!
Mikey Mite Goes to School
Mikey Mite's Big Problem

Meet Mooch

Dear Old Dumpling
A Gift from Mooch
Missing Mooch
Mooch Forever
Hang On, Mooch!
Mooch Gets Jealous
Mooch and Me
Life without Mooch

Meet the Swank Twins

Swank Talk
The Swank Prank

Meet the Loonies

Loonie Summer
Loonies Arrive

Formac Publishing Company Limited
5502 Atlantic Street, Halifax, Nova Scotia B3H 1G4
Orders: 1-800-565-1975 Fax: (902) 425-0166
www.formac.ca